MARVEL

GUARDIANS OF THE GALAXY

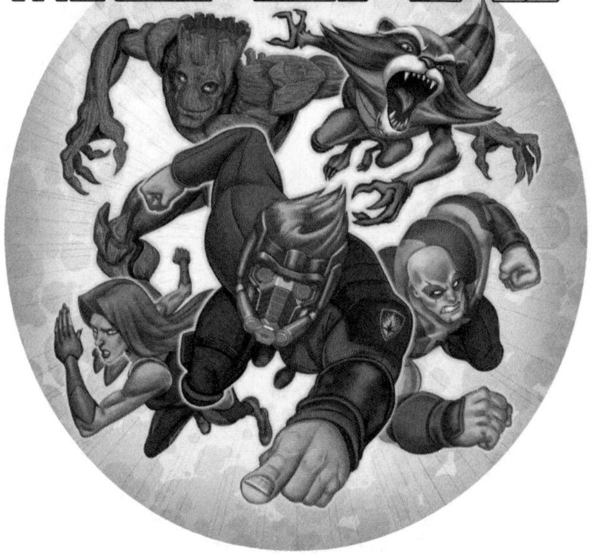

By John Sazaklis
Cover illustrated by Patrick Spaziante
Interior illustrated by Michael Borkowski and Michael Atiyeh

A GOLDEN BOOK • NEW YORK

MARVEL

marvelkids.com

All rights reserved. Published in the United States by Golden Books, an imprint of Random House Children's Books, a division of Penguin Random House LLC, 1745 Broadway, New York, NY 10019, and in Canada by Random House of Canada, a division of Penguin Random House Ltd., Toronto. Golden Books, A Golden Book, A Little Golden Book, the G colophon, and the distinctive gold spine are registered trademarks of Penguin Random House LLC.

randomhousekids.com

Educators and librarians, for a variety of teaching tools, visit us at RHTeachersLibrarians.com

ISBN 978-0-399-55096-6

Printed in the United States of America

10 9 8 7 6 5 4

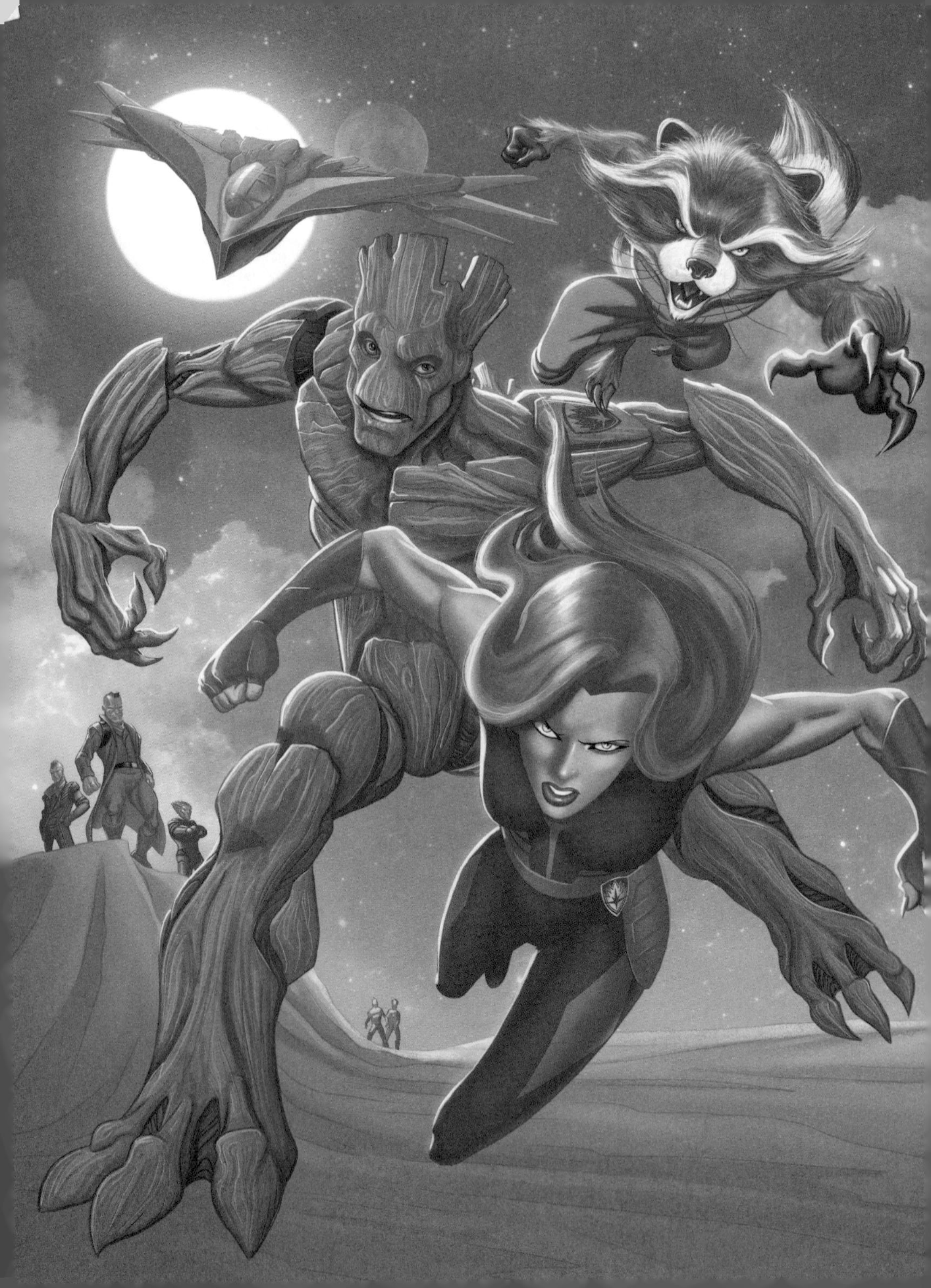

Deep in outer space, the ***GUARDIANS OF THE GALAXY*** are always ready for action! This ragtag team of heroes protects the universe from all sorts of interstellar threats.

Leading the Guardians is Peter Quill, better known as ***STAR-LORD***! He is part human and part alien. Star-Lord has amazing strength and speed, and his rocket boots blast him into battle!

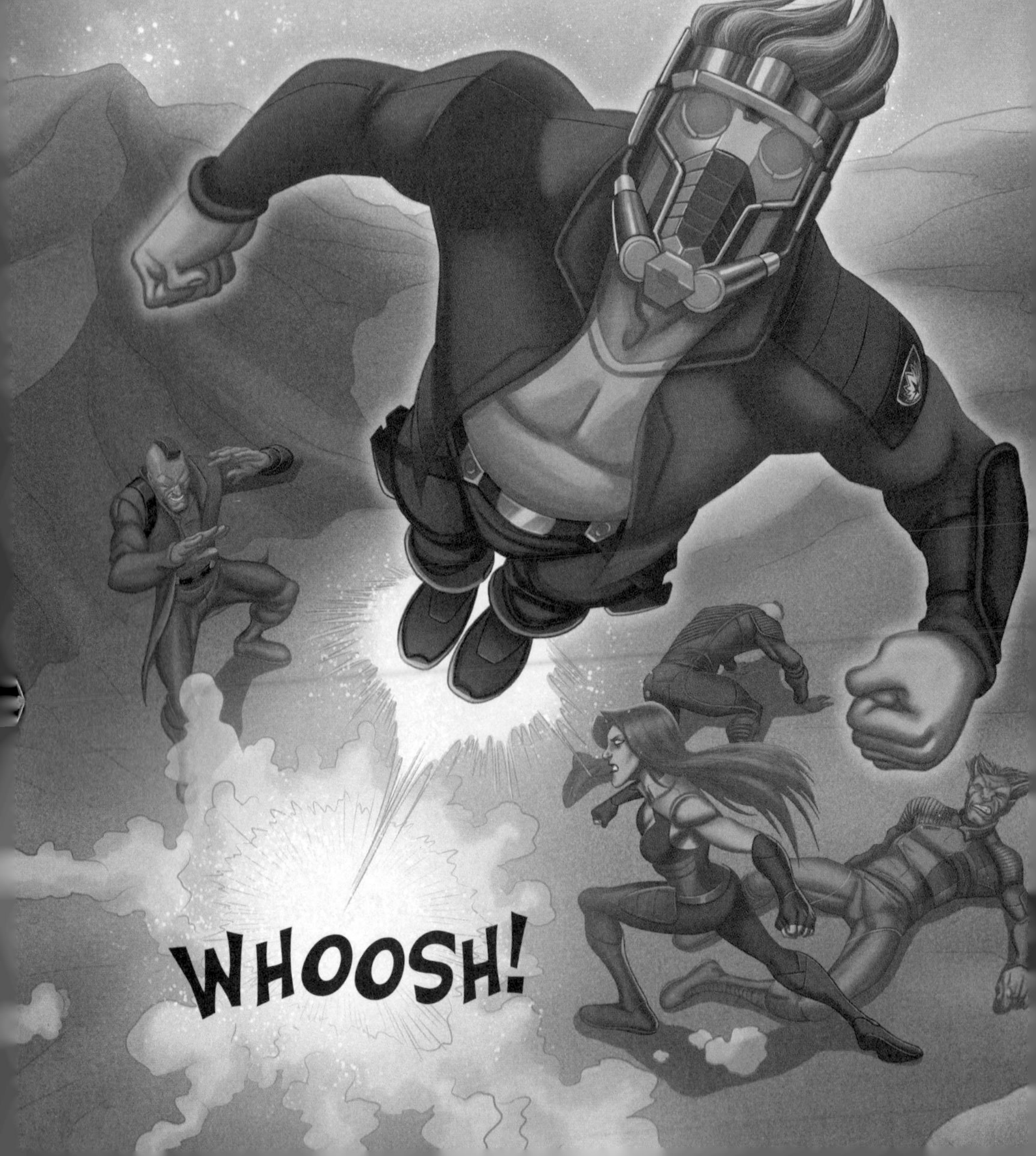
WHOOSH!

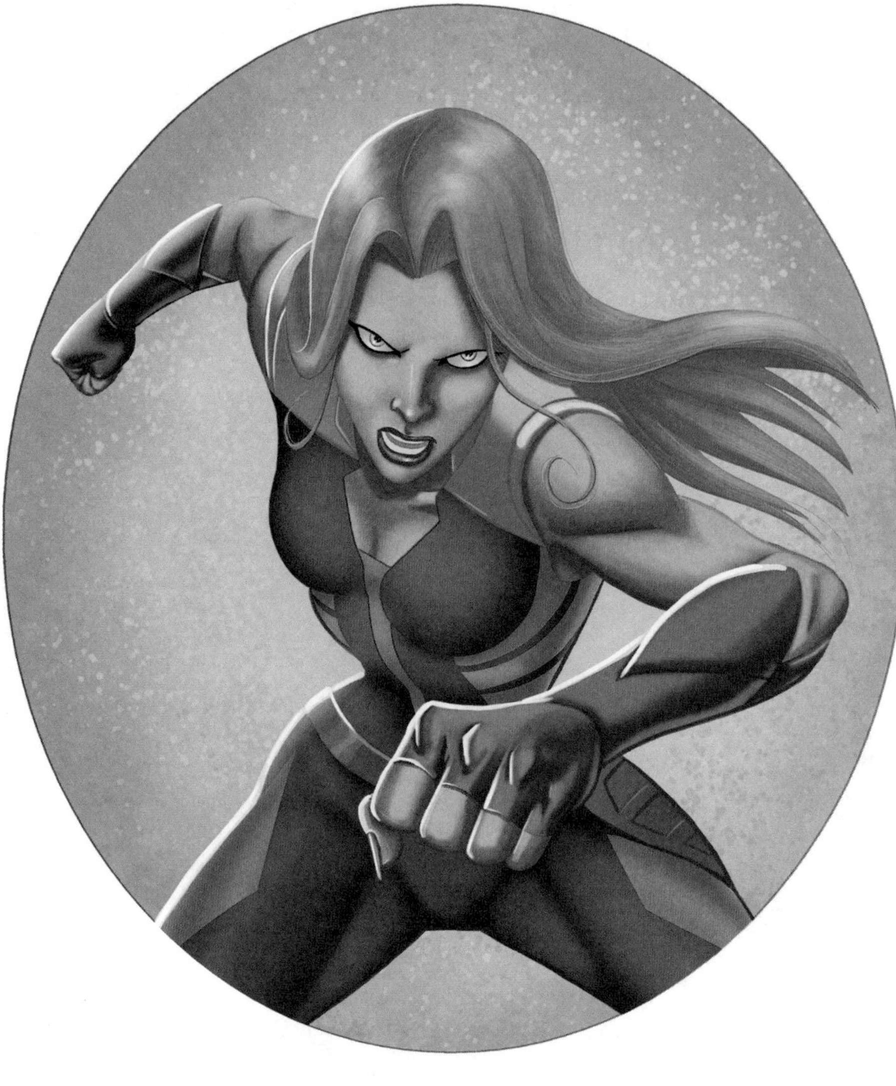

Fighting alongside Star-Lord is the green-skinned **GAMORA**. She is the last of her species—an alien race called the Zen-Whoberi. Gamora is a skilled warrior who can heal very quickly from any injury!

ROCKET RACCOON is an expert pilot. He may look cute and fuzzy, but he's no house pet! His sharp claws and enhanced senses make him tough to beat.

His best friend is **GROOT**. He is a tall, treelike creature who can control plants and grow to an immense size.

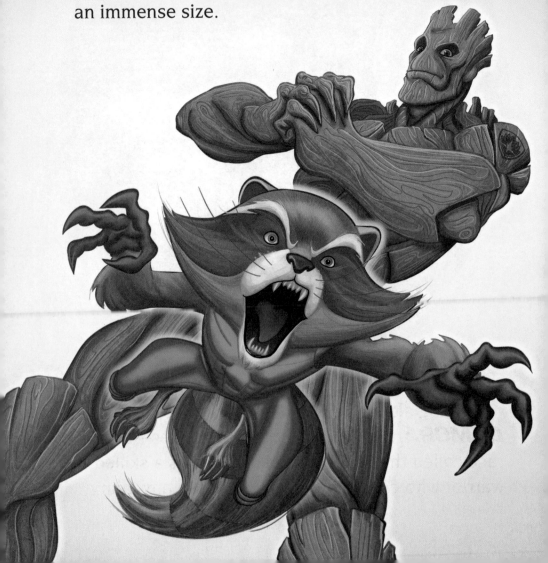

This odd couple is a powerful pair!

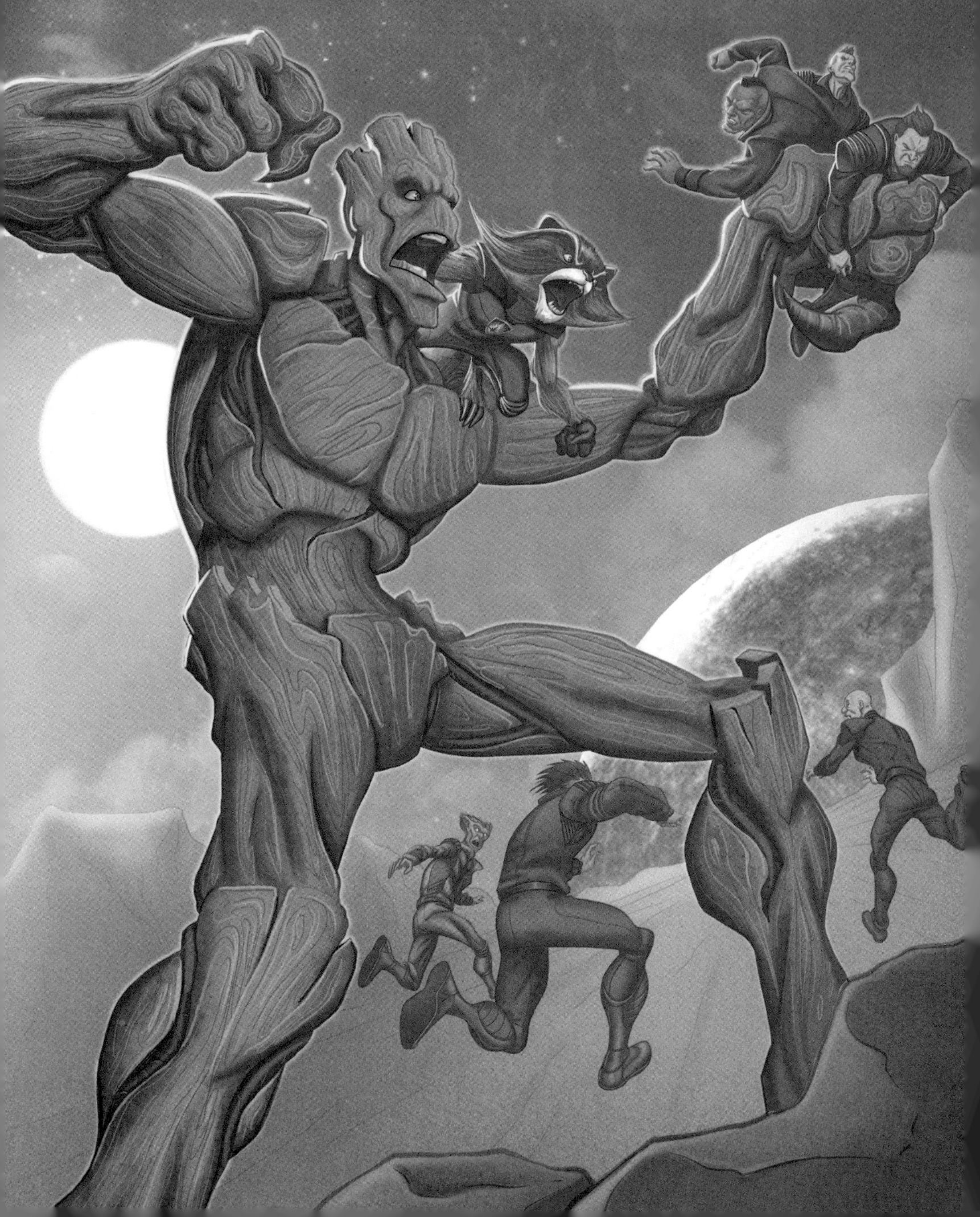

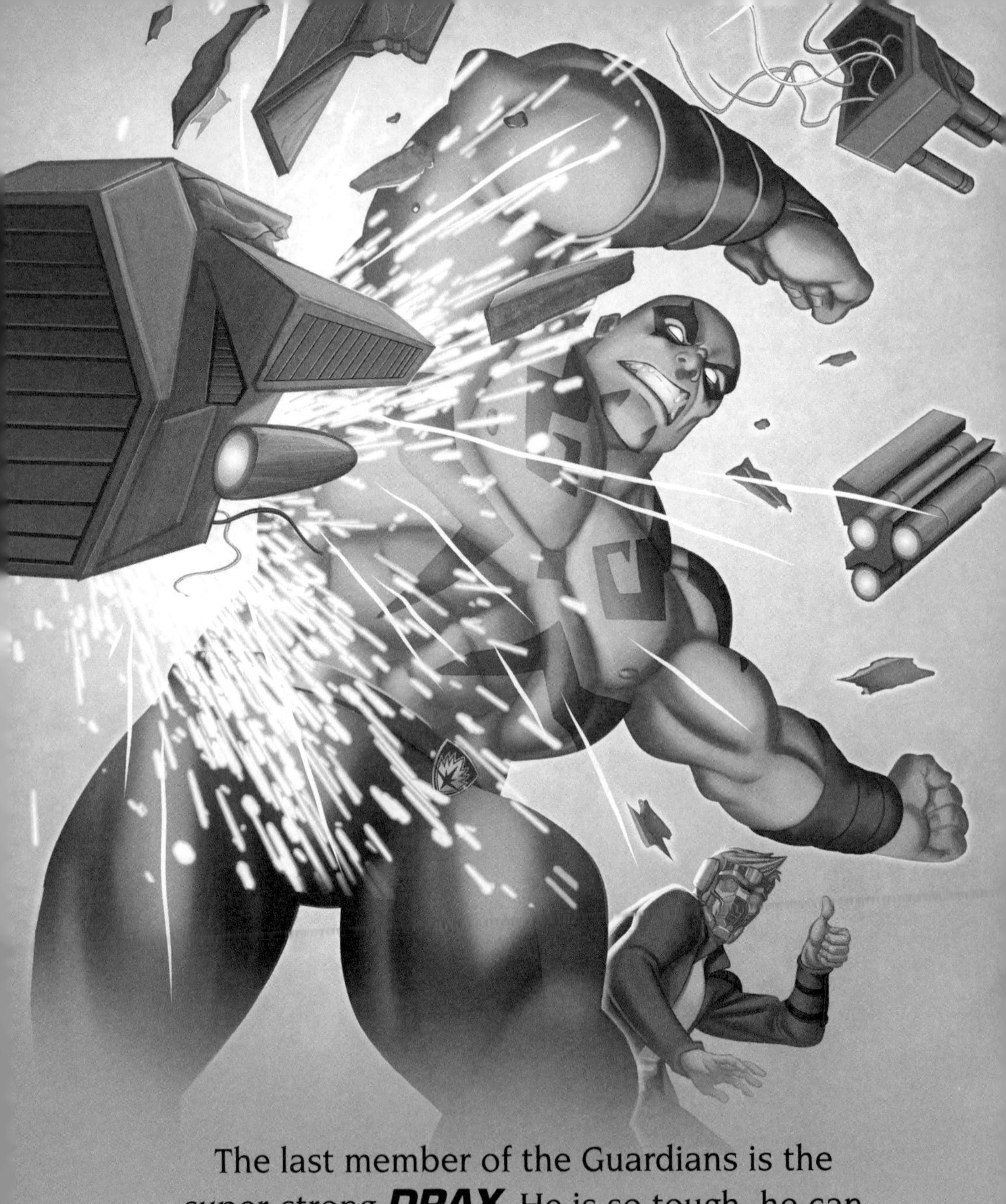

The last member of the Guardians is the super-strong ***DRAX***. He is so tough, he can survive in the extreme cold of space without air, food, or water!

The Guardians of the Galaxy search the universe for adventure in Star-Lord's spaceship, the ***MILANO***.

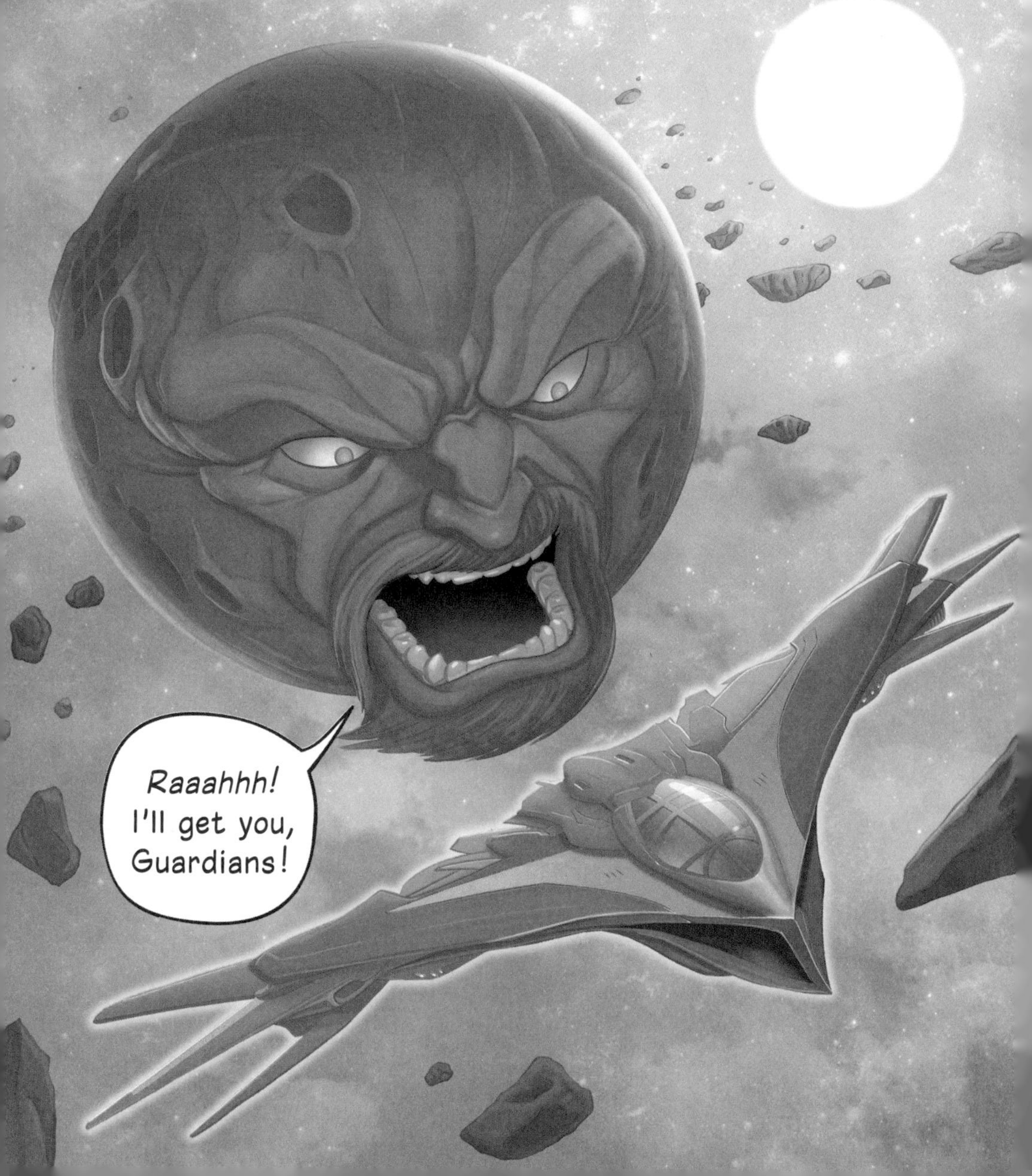
Raaahhh! I'll get you, Guardians!

The Guardians' home base is called **KNOWHERE**, and **COSMO THE DOG** is their chief of security. Cosmo helps them sniff out trouble!

The Guardians have many different frightful foes throughout the galaxy.

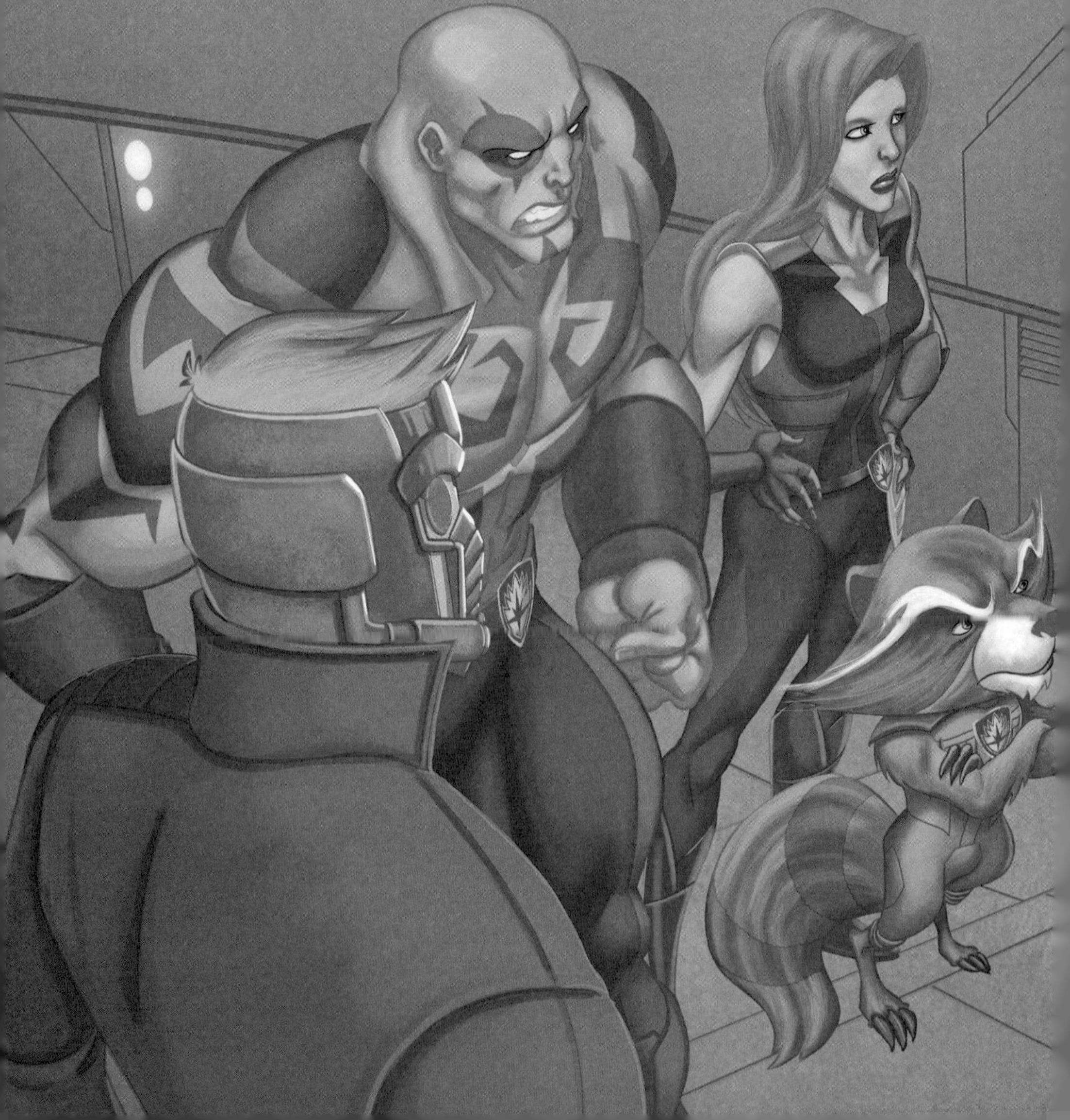

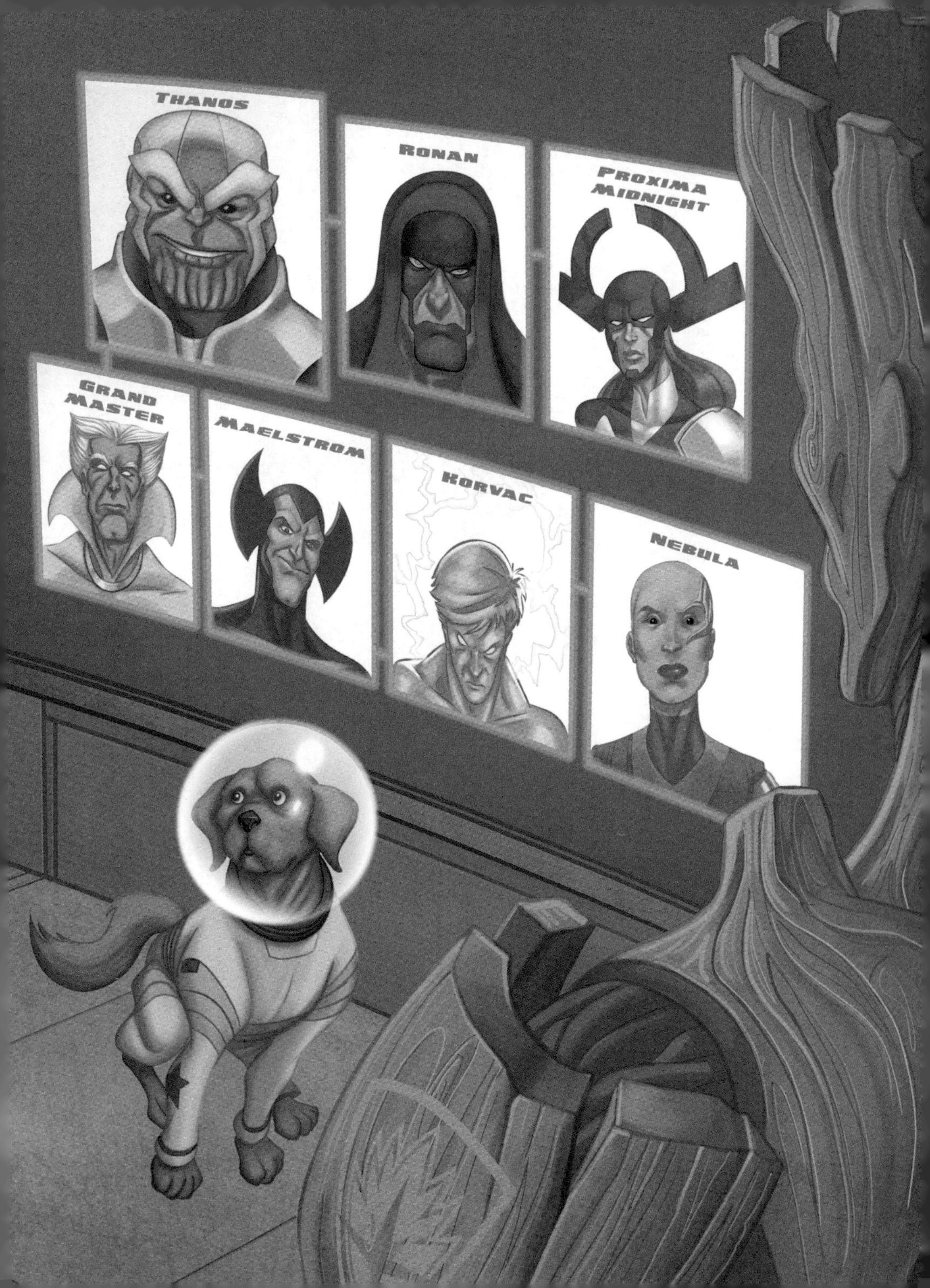

THANOS
RONAN
PROXIMA MIDNIGHT
GRAND MASTER
MAELSTROM
KORVAC
NEBULA

RONAN THE ACCUSER is a sinister soldier with super-speed, super-strength, and quick reflexes. He wields a giant hammer called the Universal Weapon. He can use it to crush almost anything!

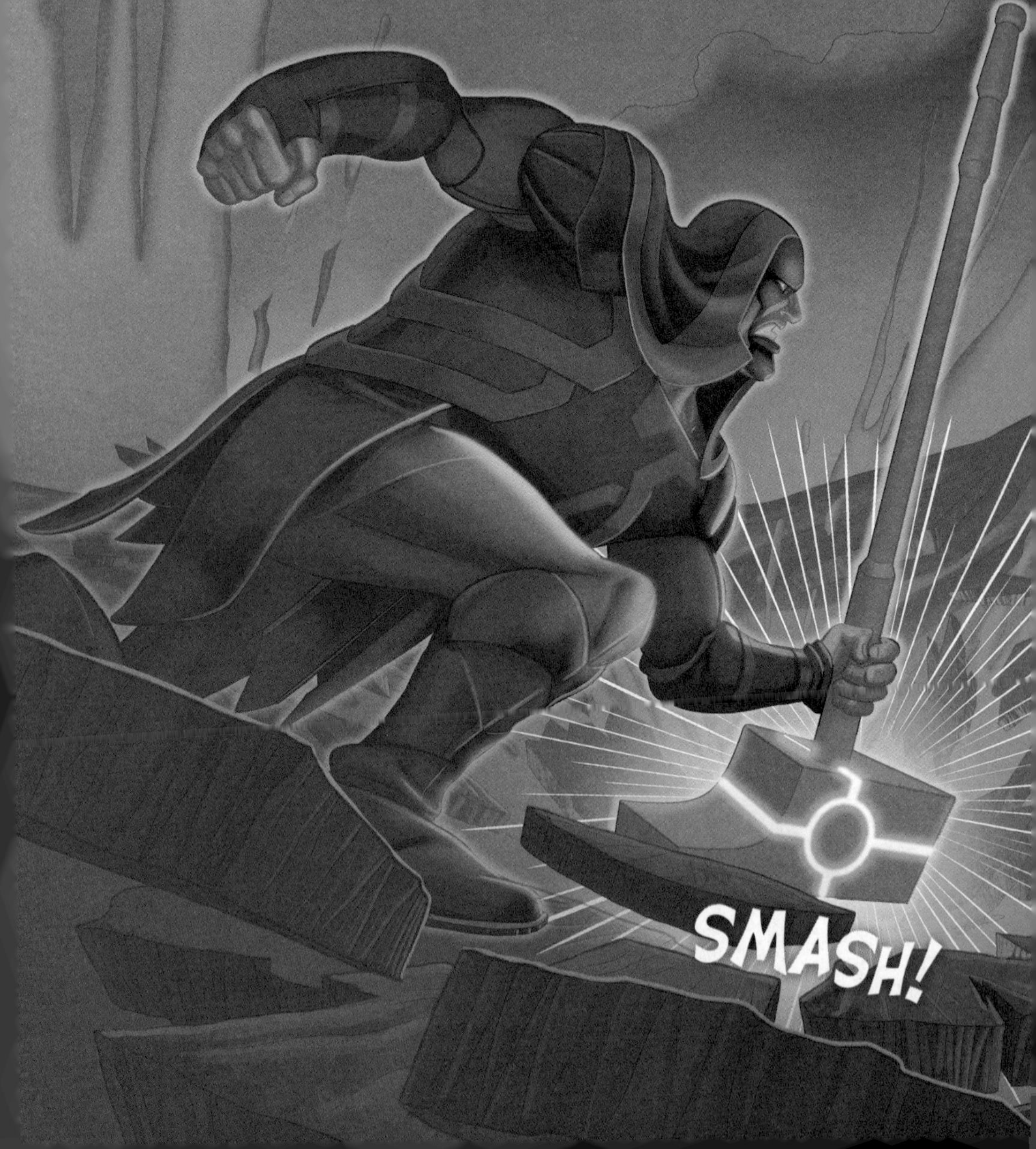
SMASH!

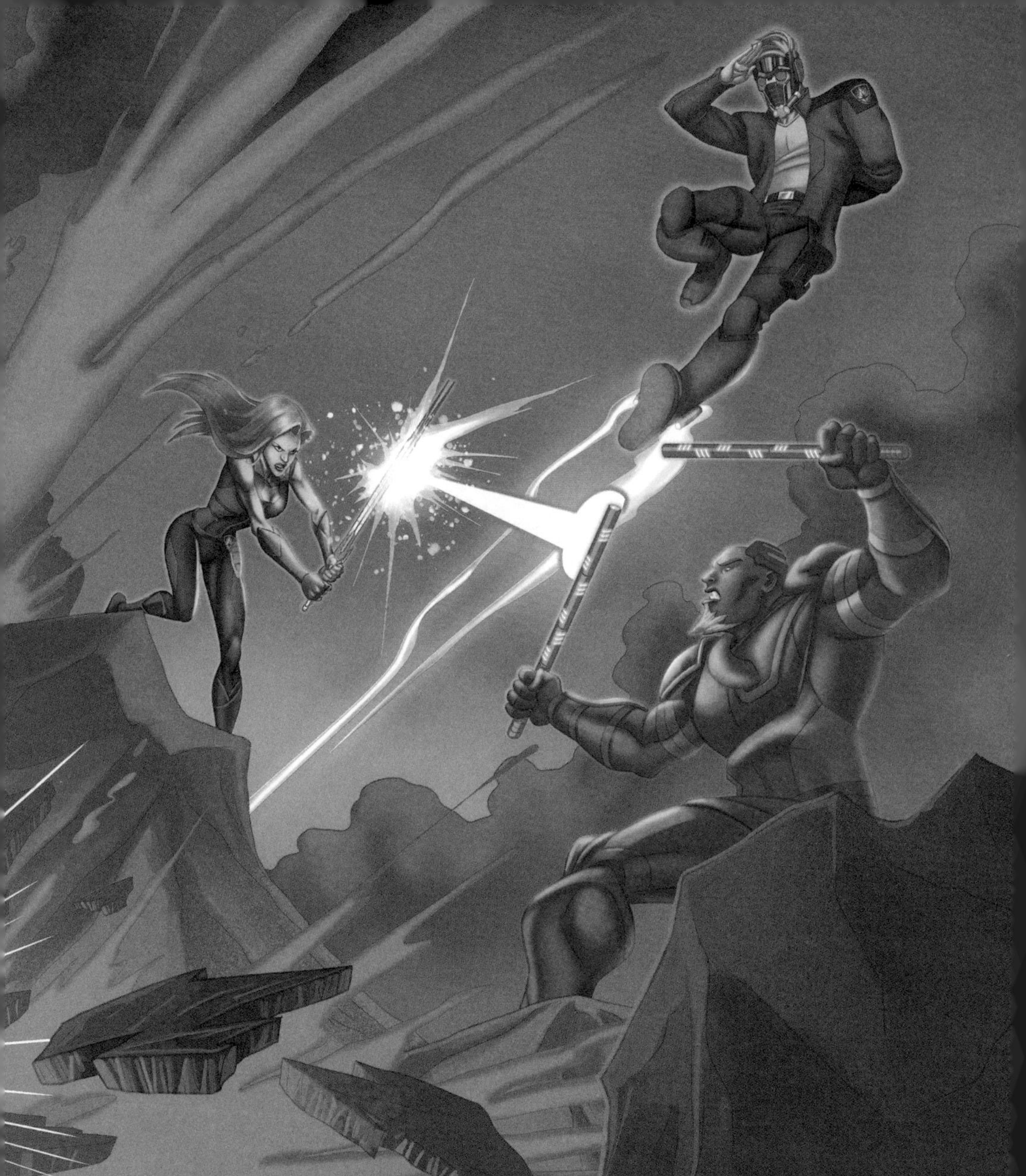

Like Ronan, ***KORATH THE PURSUER*** is a member of the alien Kree race. He carries two batons that fire powerful bolts of energy.

The **COLLECTOR** is an ancient being who travels the universe acquiring alien artifacts—especially those with great power!

Unfortunately for the Collector and the fearsome tiger man **TITUS**, Rocket Raccoon and Groot don't play by his rules.

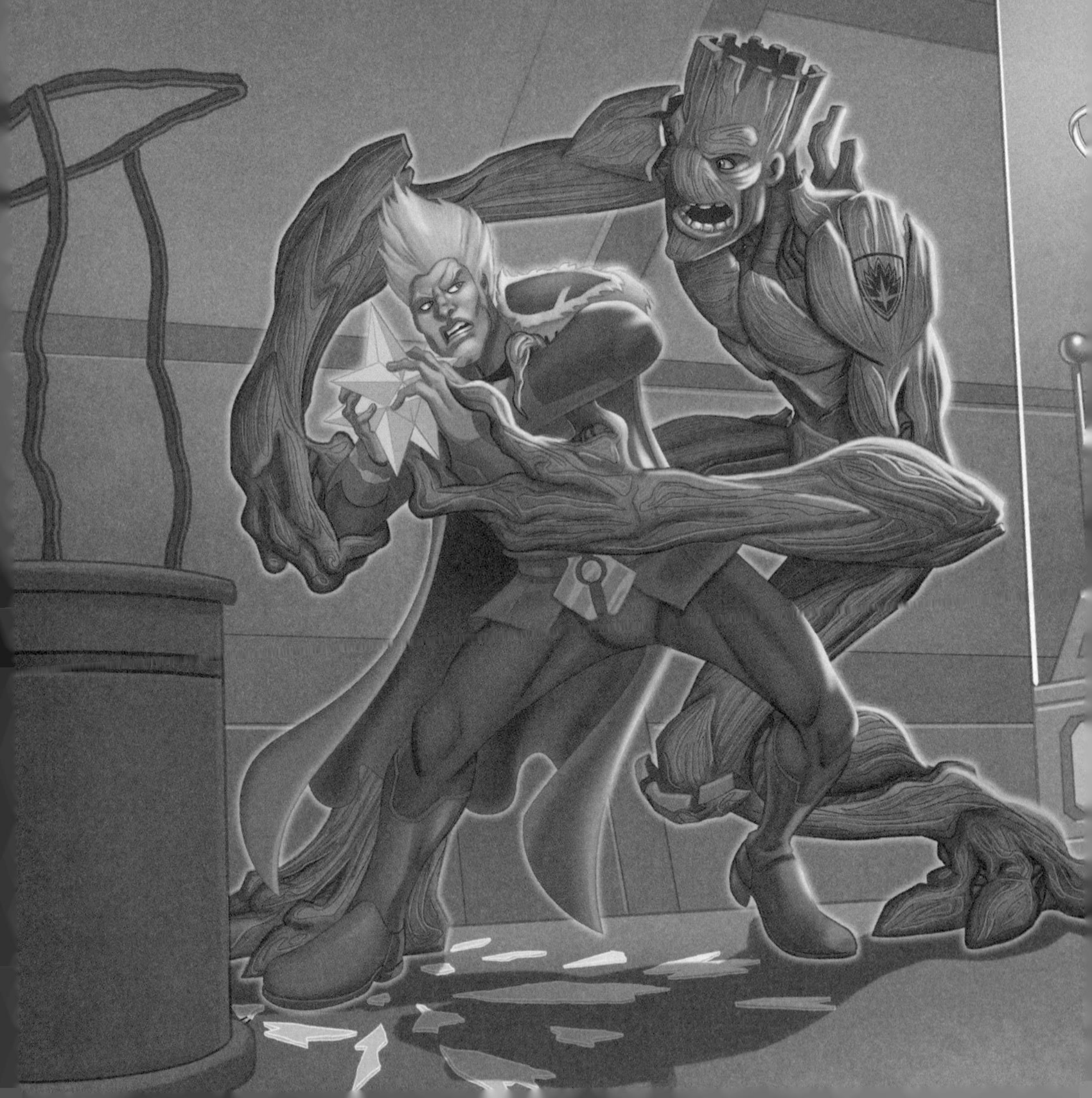

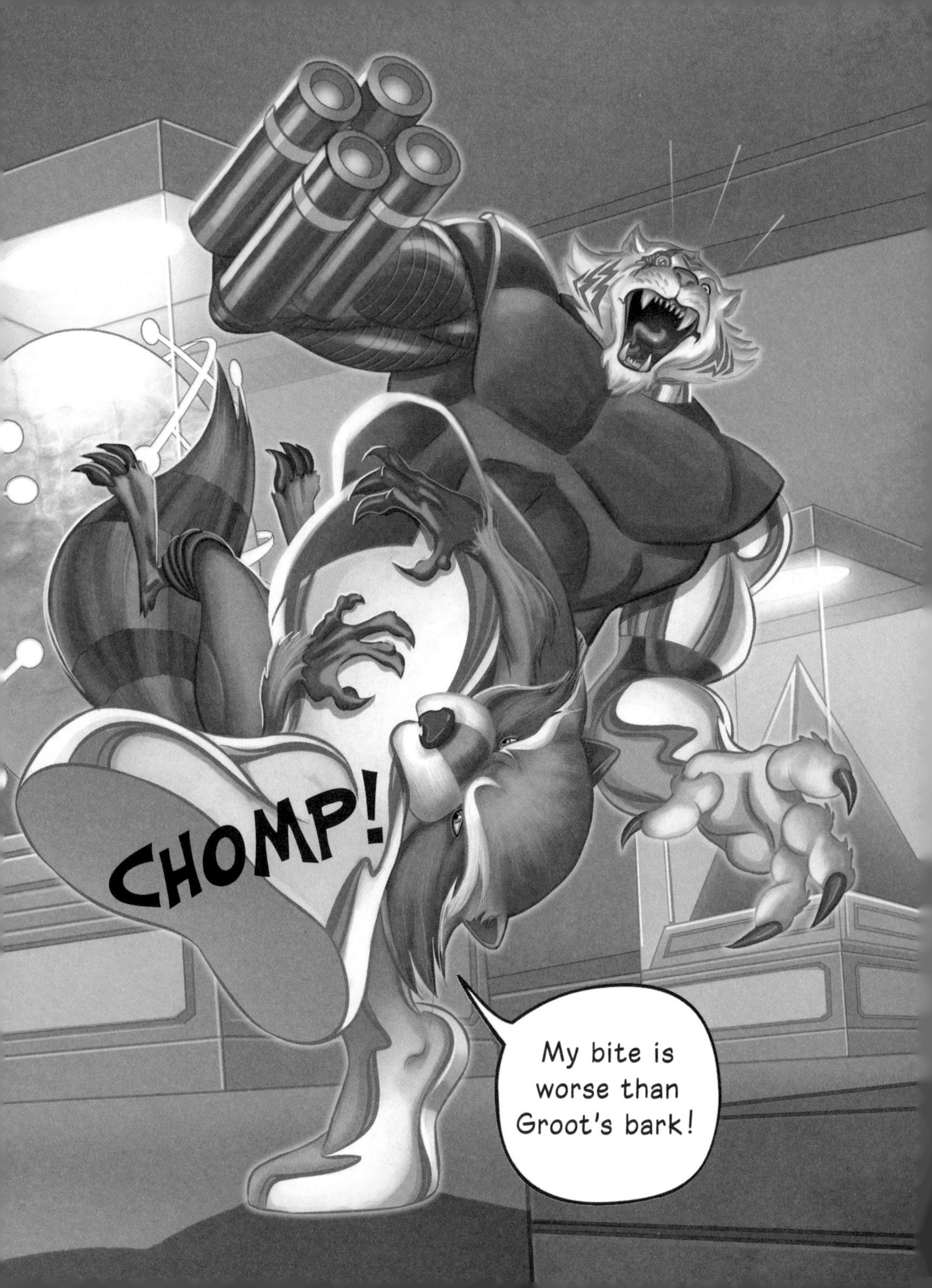
CHOMP!
My bite is worse than Groot's bark!

Feared across the galaxy, the space pirate **NEBULA** is a cyborg. She may be part machine, but she's *all* trouble for the Guardians—and the bad guys, too!

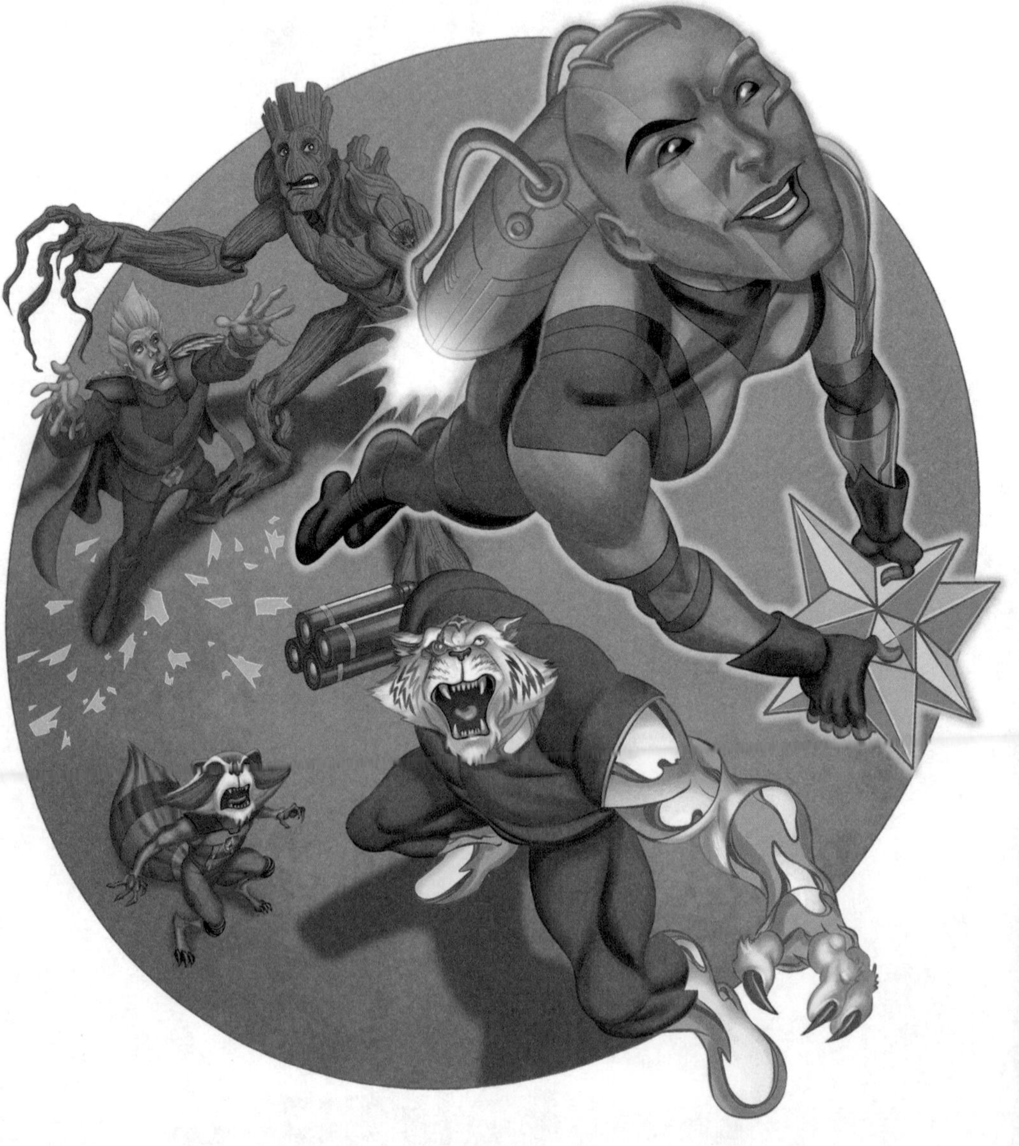

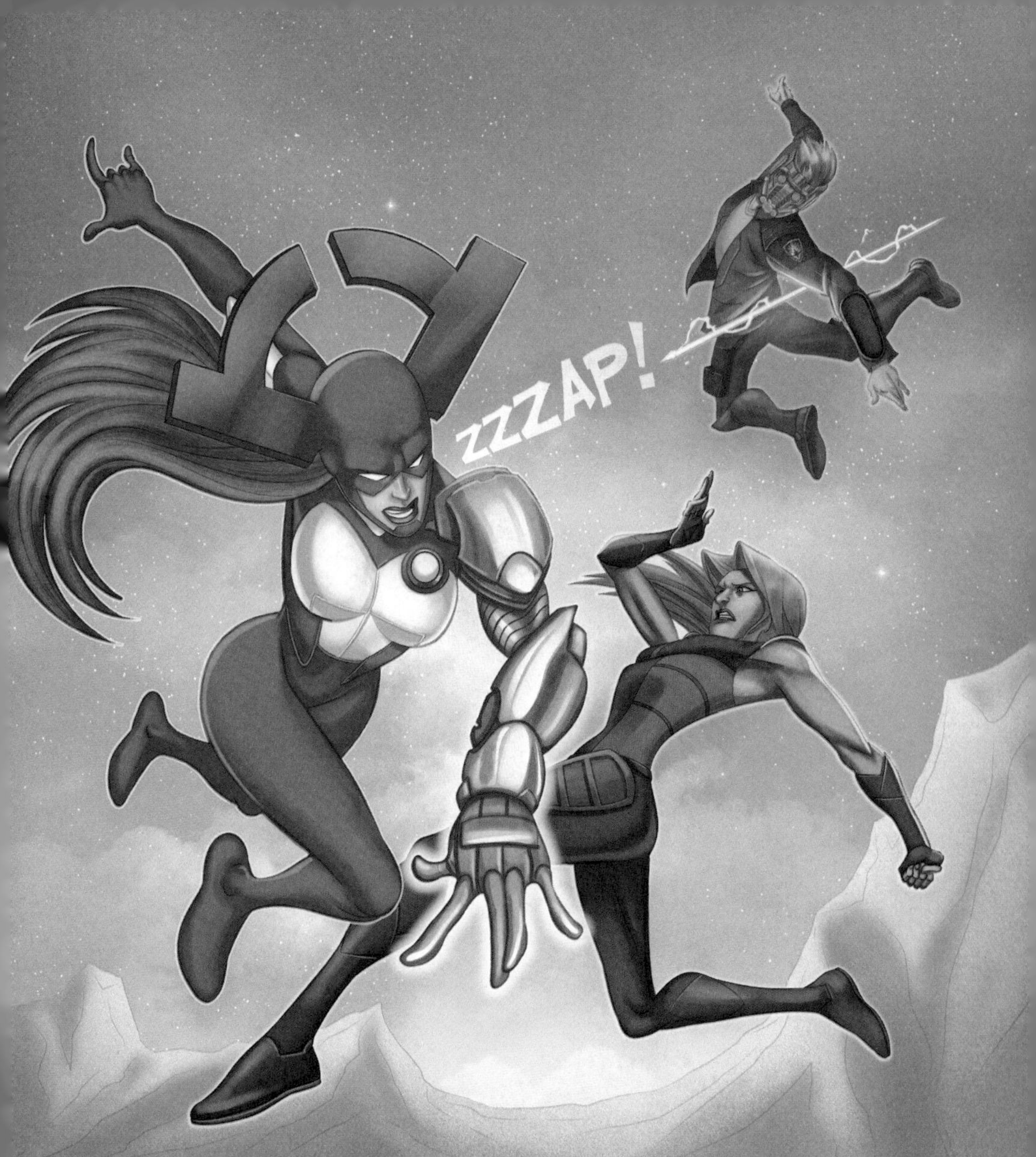
ZZZAP!

PROXIMA MIDNIGHT is a master of hand-to-hand combat. Her deadliest weapon is a spear made from pure star energy.

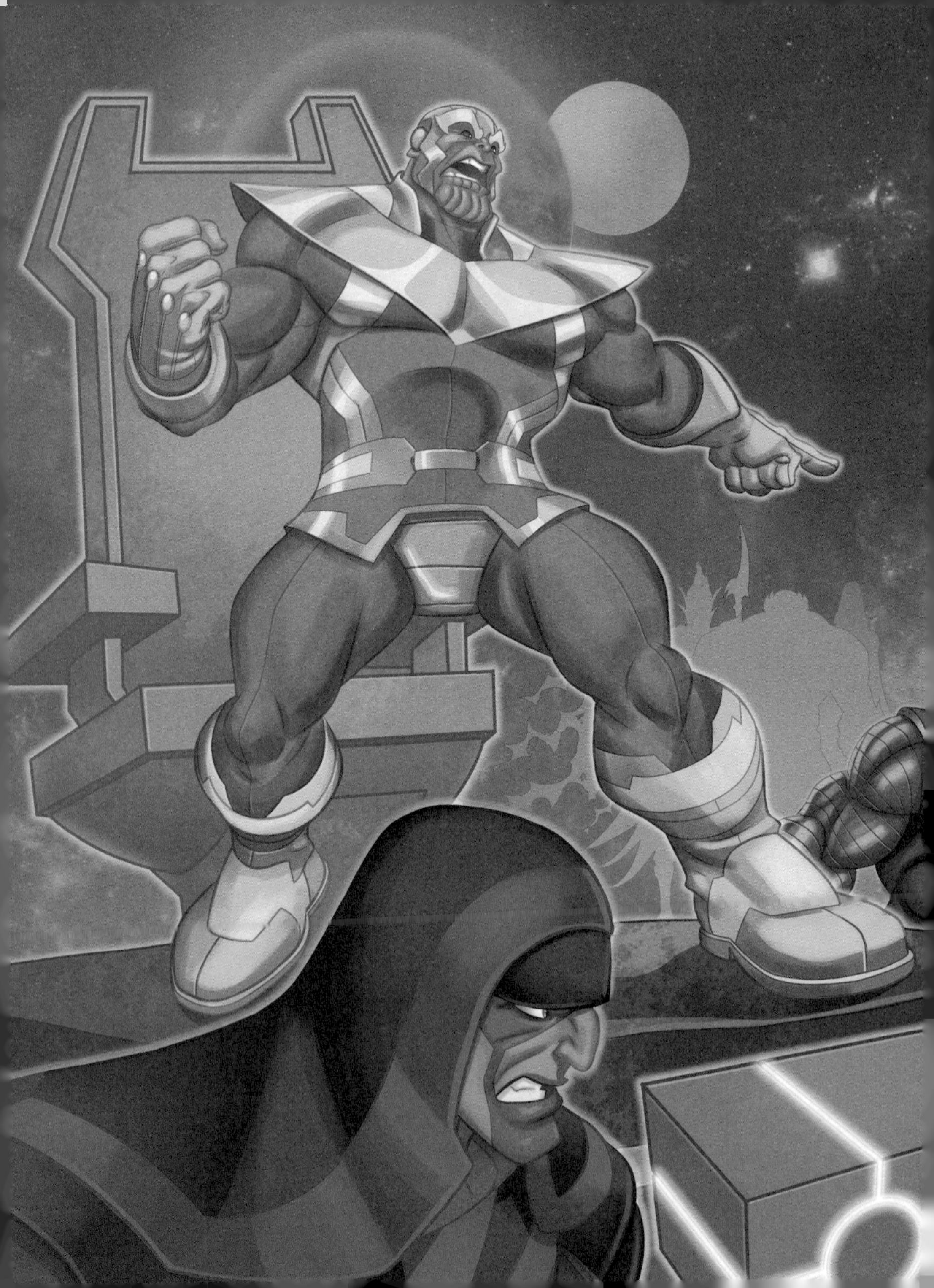

Possibly the greatest menace to the galaxy is **THANOS**. His life's goal is to control the entire universe!

Thanos has teamed up with other villains to try to defeat the Guardians of the Galaxy.

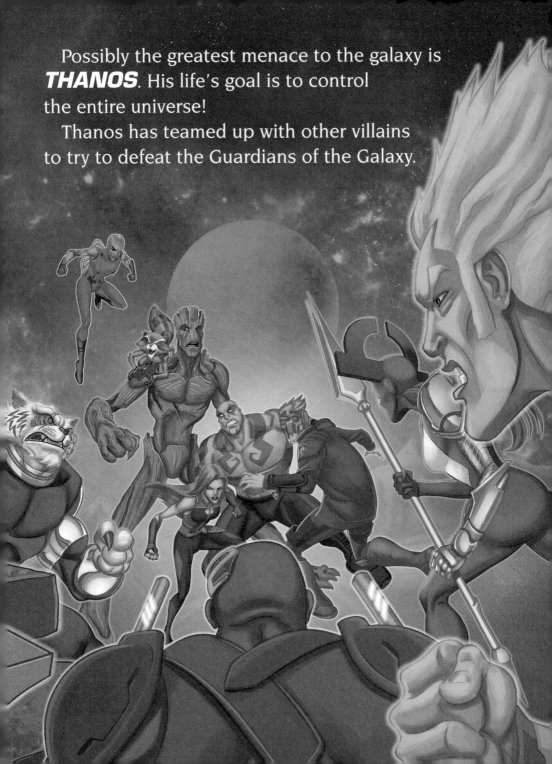

The monstrous **BLACK DWARF**, the energy-blade-wielding **CORVUS GLAIVE**, and the mind-eating telepath **SUPERGIANT** are also minions of Thanos.

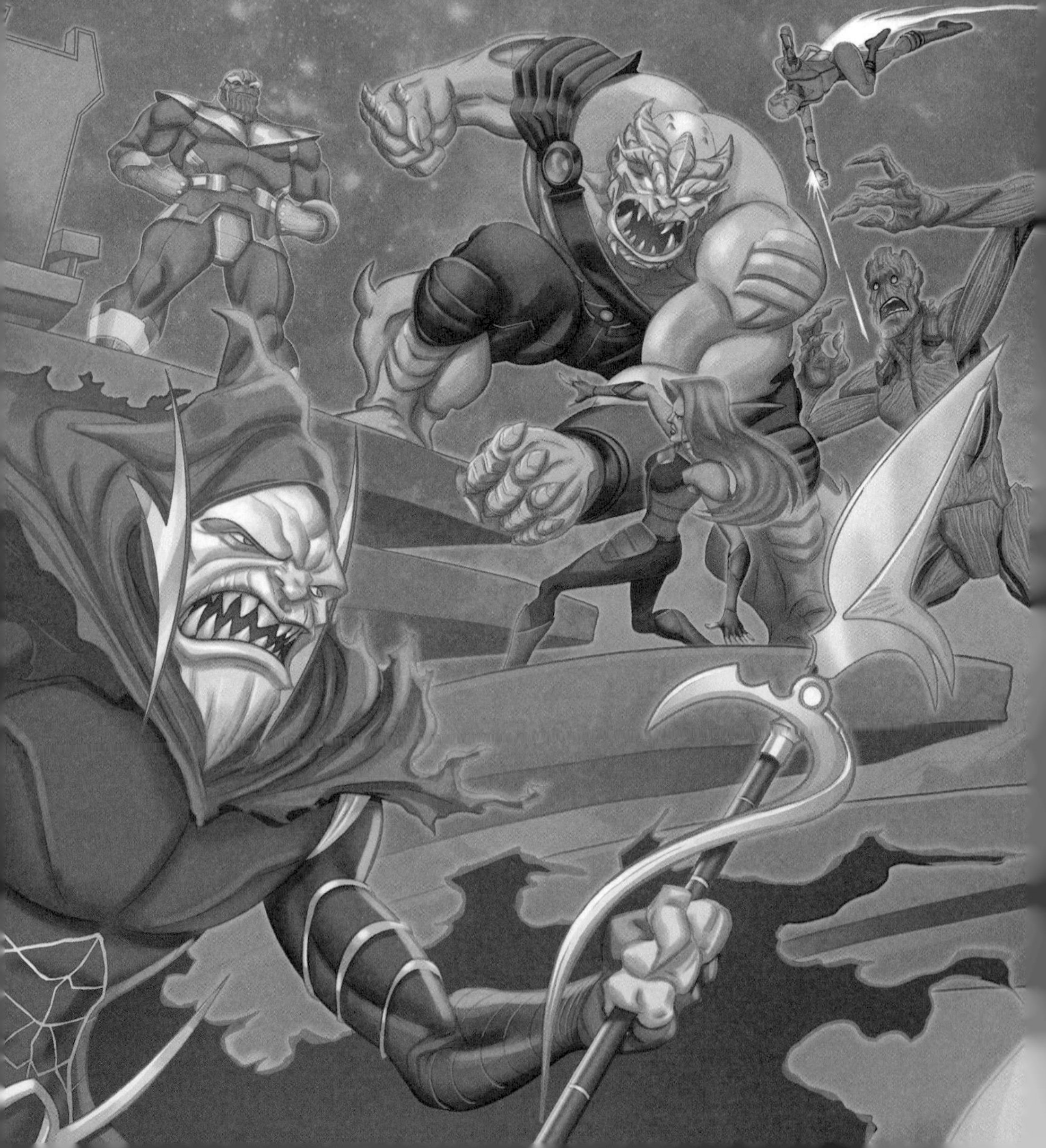

With all these powerful henchmen at his side, Thanos thinks he is invulnerable . . . but the Guardians plan to prove him wrong.

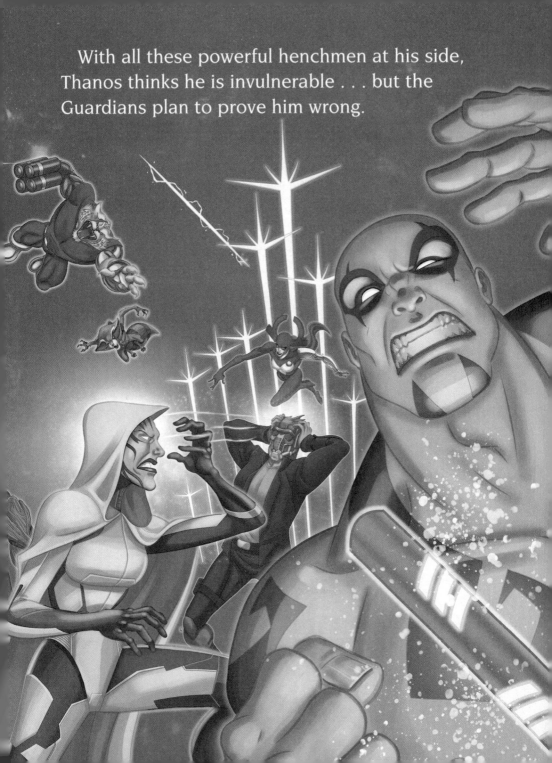

When the Guardians of the Galaxy face off against Thanos and his terrible team, the fight is fierce, but good ultimately overpowers evil.

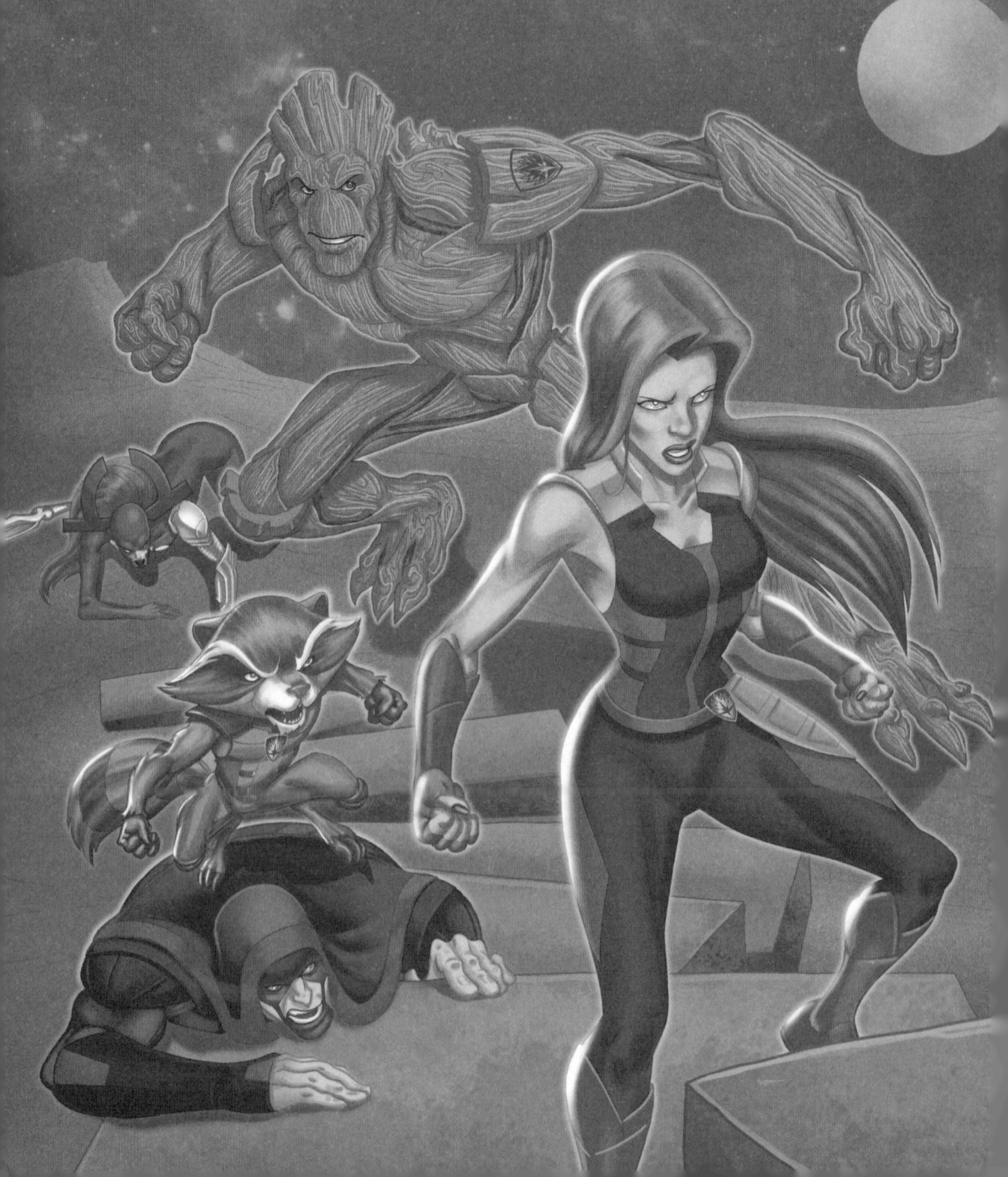

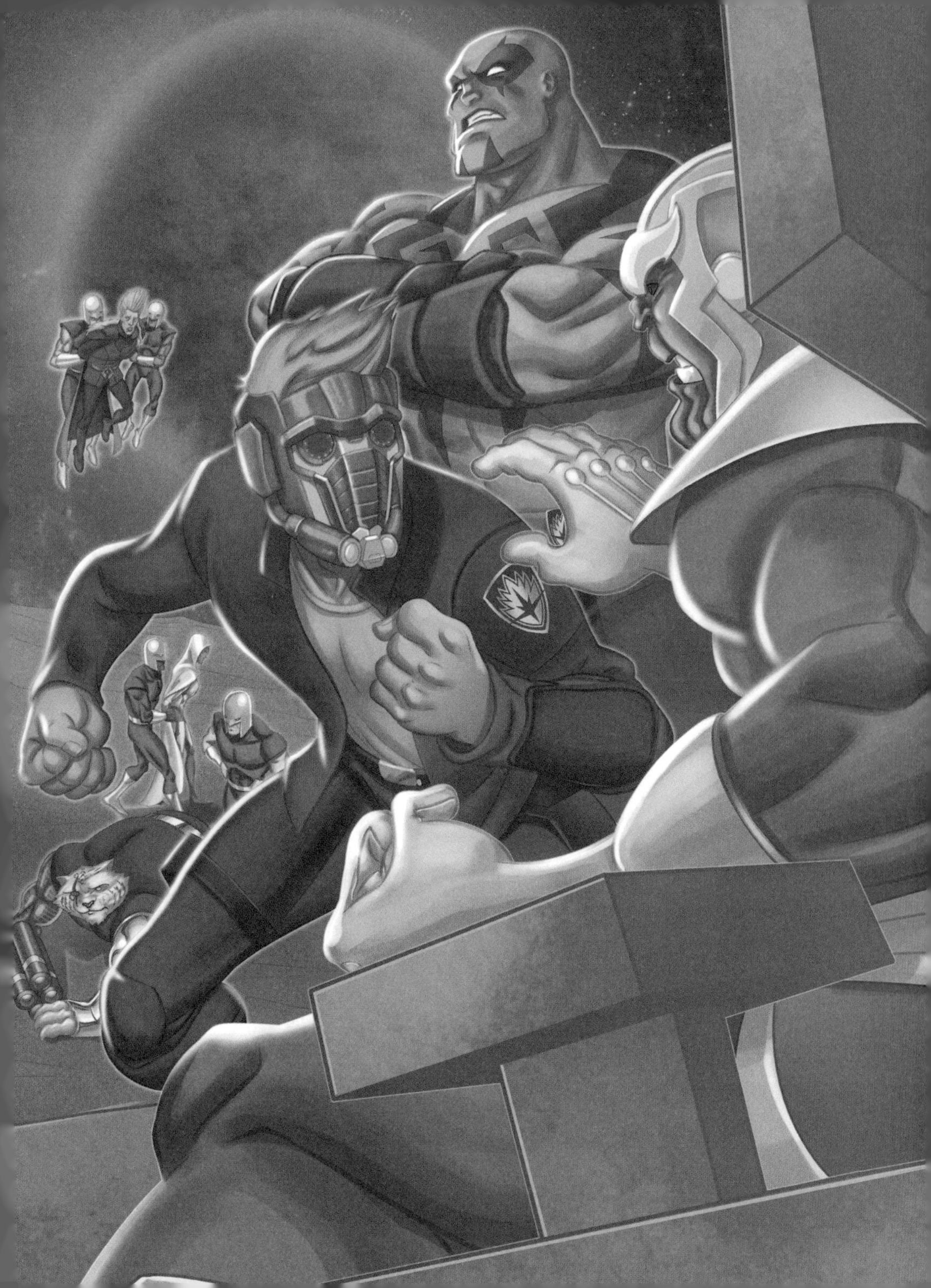

With the battle won, Star-Lord and his friends head home. The universe will always be safe under the protection of the Guardians of the Galaxy.

GO, GUARDIANS, GO!

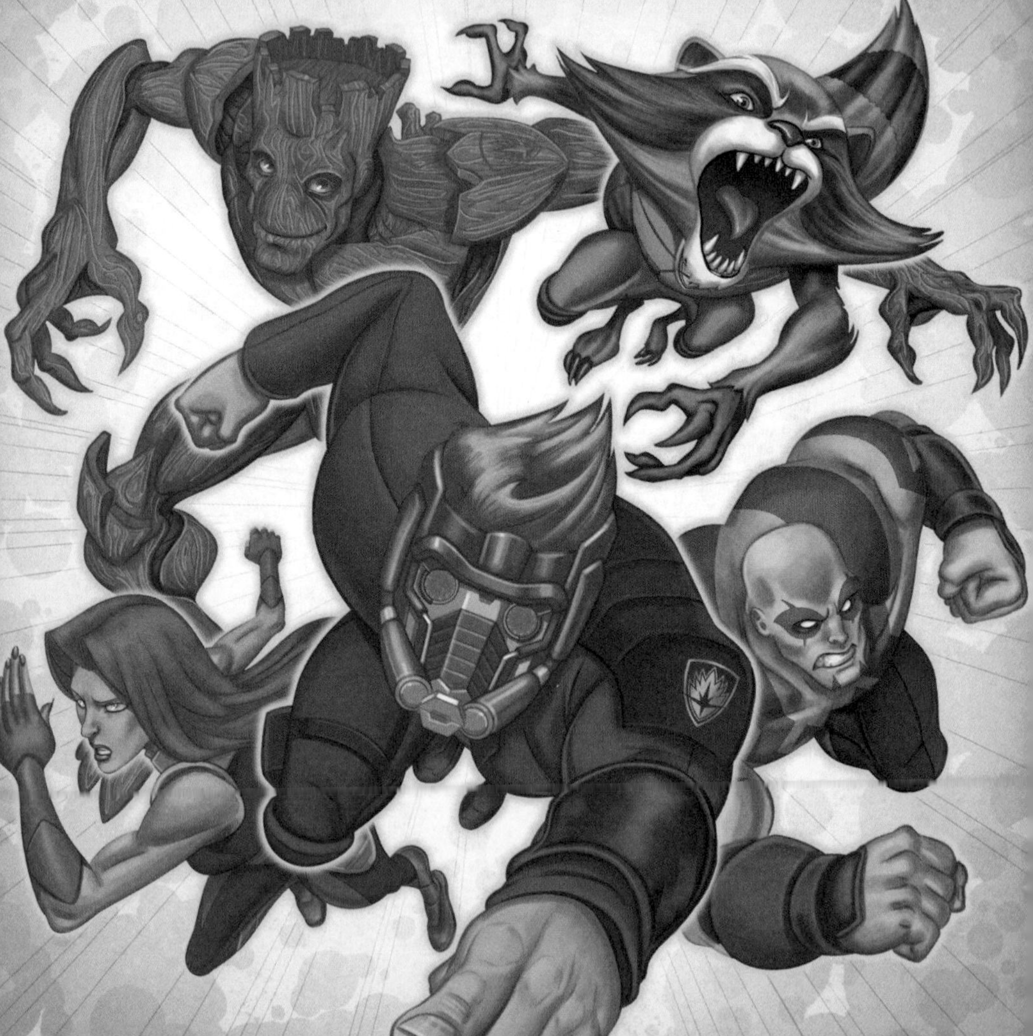